JAKE MADDOX
GRAPHIC NOVELS

STONE ARCH BOOKS
a capstone imprint

BASKETBALL
BIG SHOTS

TABLE OF CONTENTS

VIPER
15

Text by Brandon Terrell

Art by Berenice Muñiz

Color by Armando Ramirez

Lettering by Jaymes Reed

THE STARTING LINEUP

bonus
COACH ROGERS

Kidz
COOK
BRENTON SPOONER

VIPERS
22
CHARLIE BEST

Hey there. I'm Henry Watson. My friends call me Hank.

What? My story? You really wanna hear my story? Okay.

So it starts like this.

There are two things I love more than anything in the world. The first is basketball.

I've been playing hoops for as long as I can remember.

But my other passion? The other thing I've been doing since I don't know when? Cooking.

My gramma let me watch her in the kitchen. It was like magic, seeing how she made the most delicious food from simple ingredients.
Now don't you over-whisk the batter, though, or your pancakes won't be fluffy.

I know what you're thinking. Basketball? Cooking? They couldn't be more different.
22
But they've actually got a lot in common.

Both basketball and cooking need certain elements for success.
Abdi, set a pick for Hank, and Hank, you take it to the hoop.

First, you need a recipe. Like Coach Rogers's playbook . . .
WHUMP!

. . . or the recipe book gramma left me when she died.
Without a gameplan, you don't know if you'll be tasting sweet victory or bitter defeat.

Then you have to make sure you have the right ingredients.
SWISH!

SLAP!
Easy bucket, dude.
Great pick, Abdi!

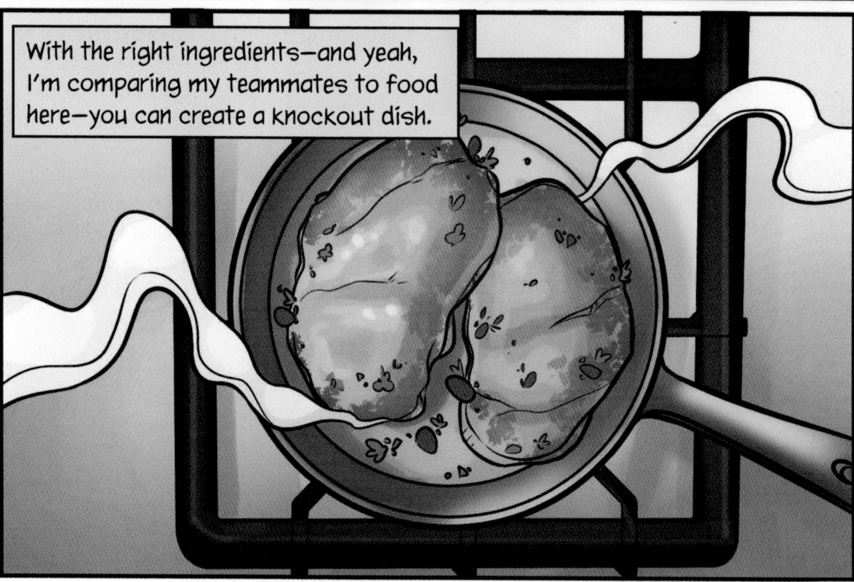
With the right ingredients—and yeah, I'm comparing my teammates to food here—you can create a knockout dish.

Great win, team!
When the right ingredients work well together, you can achieve great success. Both on the court . . .
VIPERS
15

. . . and in the kitchen.

Sorry if you can hear my stomach rumbling. Just talking about food makes me hungry.
So anyway, our team, the Bridgeton Vipers, was off to a great start.
Of course, what I didn't know was that our season was about to become a recipe for disaster.

Hey! Who wants to celebrate this win in style? I'm thinking double cheeseburgers, chocolate malts you can dip your fries into . . .
I'm in!
Sounds excelenté.

Whaddaya say, Hank? You in?

Nah. Sorry, guys. I promised my mom I'd make her my famous spaghetti. It's a tradition after the first game of the season.
Maybe next time.

Pfff, whatever, Mr. Chef Man.

I mean, you'd think it'd be weird, telling the guys I was off to cook dinner for my family.
But they all knew I liked to cook. It wasn't a big deal.

At least, not that night. Not when the season started. But . . .
. . . sometimes things change.

That night I tried a new recipe for spaghetti alla carbonara. It was posted online by a food blogger I followed—

—legendary chef (and my culinary hero), Brenton Spooner.
SPAGHETTI ALLA CARBONARA
BRENTON SPOONER
INGREDIENTS
12 oz. spaghetti
Kosher salt
3 large eggs
1 c. freshly grated Parmesan
8 slices bacon
2 cloves garlic, minced
Freshly ground black pepper
Extra-virgin olive oil (optional), for garnish
DIRECTIONS
1 In a large pot of salted boiling water, cook spaghetti according to package directions until al dente. Drain, reserving 1 cup pasta water.
2 In a medium bowl, whisk eggs and Parmesan until combined.
3 Meanwhile, in a large skillet over medium heat, cook bacon until crispy, about 8 minutes. Reserve fat in skillet and transfer slices to a paper towel-lined plate to drain.

Come on now, Sadie! There's only five minutes left to finish your dish!
Spooner hosted KidzCook, a cooking competition show. I'd actually sent in an audition tape to be a contestant but hadn't heard back.
Kidz COOK

In order to keep myself from obsessing about the audition, I spent my time either on the court or in the kitchen.

Hey-ya! Whatcha cookin' tonight?
Spaghetti alla carbonara.
Smells yummy!
Put away the work, Dad. Time to eat. 
Okay, okay.
Mom still at the office?

Yep. Just the three of us tonight. Smells delicious as usual, champ.

It's here! Oh man, they wrote back to me about my audition tape!

Here, Pop. You open it. I can't.

You okay, kiddo?
Yeah. Fine. I'm fine. Do I look fine? Just read it.
RIIIPP

"Dear Mr. Watson, Thank you for sending us your audition tape.
We have received over 5,000 entries, and only a select hundred young chefs will be chosen to cook in a live audition for Brenton Spooner.
Of those chefs, 20 will be given a golden spatula, and the chance to become a KidzCook champion."

"Congratulations, Mr. Watson. You have been chosen for the live auditions!"
ALRIGHT! Yes!
Eeekk!

I'd done it.
I'd earned a chance to cook a meal for my idol.

If all went well, I'd make it onto the show.
Needless to say, I was jazzed the next day.

TAP!
The excitement stayed with me. Whatever came my way . . .

WHUMP!
. . . I felt like I could handle it.

So when we played our next game against the Hurricanes, I could barely feel my sneakers on the court.
HURRICANES
VIPERS

VIPERS
THUNK!

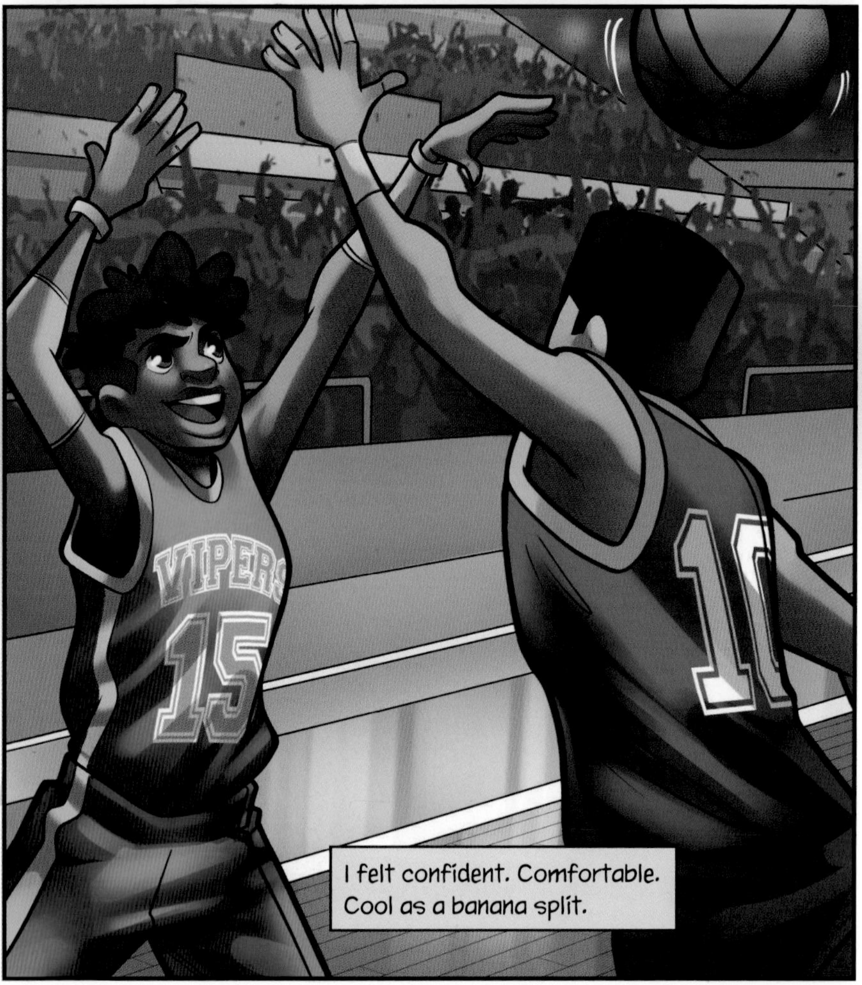

I felt confident. Comfortable.
Cool as a banana split.

SWISH!

Nice hoop. You're in the zone, man!

And man, were we cooking in that game!

SWISH!

Great work out there, team. Charlie, nice shot.

Thanks, Coach.

By the end of the first half, we were up by 25 points.

We did just that. We played the second half with the same intensity as we had at tip-off.
Each one of us, every ingredient, were doing our part.

Oof.

HURRICANES
4
We gave it our all until the final buzzer.

SWISH!

Good job.
Way to go.
Good game.

Good game? Nah. Try GREAT game!
What made it even better was that I planned to tell my team about the KidzCook audition.
When Charlie invited us to his house for movie night, I thought it was the perfect chance to tell the team.
SPACE WARS
FAST, FAST, FASTER!
Make yourselves at home, fellas. Pizza's been ordered; pool table is racked and ready.
I made homemade cookies to share with the guys and everything.
Hey, guys. I brought a snack.

I made gramma's special chocolate chip cookies. I baked them for every special event in my life.

Yes—cookie time!

I've got some fun news to share with you guys.

Yeah? What is it?

I auditioned for the next season of KidzCook . . .

. . . and they want me to cook live for Brenton Spooner! Can you believe it?

Yeah, it was a little over the top. But I was excited.
It was pretty cool news to share with my friends.

Whoa.
Nice
work!
Congrats,
man! That's
so cool.

In fact, I was so jazzed that I couldn't sleep that night.
All I could think about was what to
cook for the KidzCook audition.

I wondered which dish would make gramma proud.
RECIPE
Focaccia
DIRECTIONS
INGREDIENTS

Over the next few days, I tried my hand at a bunch of gramma's recipes.
Chicken pot pie. Filet mignon and potato purée. Raspberry tarts.
I wanted to make something that would make Brenton Spooner's taste buds sing.

But nothing seemed like the right dish.

The closer it came to the live audition . . .
CHOP! CHOP! CHOP!

. . . the more nervous I got.

And being nervous is never a good thing. In the kitchen or on the court. Because if you lose focus or get distracted . . .

. . . you'll get burned.

AHHHHH!!!!

CLANG!

Yeah, I'm—ouch—fine. I just lost focus for a second.
WHOOSH!

The burn on my hand stung something fierce.
I'll get the burn cream and bandages, Hank.

It's fine now.
But we had an important game the day after I burned my hand.
And I was embarrassed to tell my teammates.

So I didn't say anything. I just took off the bandages and acted like nothing had happened.
All right, boys! Let's go out there and win!

For some reason, I thought things were going to be fine.

Rondo! I'm open!
But that was before I got the ball.

When Rondo sent a hard chest pass to me . . .
VIPERS
. . . it felt like a hot knife stabbed my hand.
AGGHH!
THWACK!
VIPERS
My kitchen disaster led to other problems for me on the court too.

I did everything I could to hide my injury. I tried dribbling just with my left hand.
FERRETS
17

But I didn't have the same ball control.
FERRETS
THWACK!

Our opponents took advantage of every mistake I made.
FERRETS
17
22

What's going on out there, Watson? Am I gonna have to bench you?
No, Coach. I'm fine.
But I wasn't. Every dribble, rebound, and jump shot hurt.

No matter how hard I tried, the ball wouldn't go where I wanted it to.
VIPERS
15

THUNK!

And I couldn't hide my injured hand anymore.

Watson, what's up? Turnovers? Missed shots? Dropped passes? That's not like you. What's going on?

I . . . I burned my shooting hand last night. It hurts pretty bad.

How'd it happen?

It was a cooking accident. I've been spending a lot of time practicing for my KidzCook audition.

KidzCook? We're losing this game because of that cooking show you're always talking about?
Unbelievable!

If you can't give this team everything you've got, maybe you shouldn't even be on the court!
Sorry, guys.

Coach tried to be supportive. "Accidents happen," he said. "Just try to do the best you can."

But it was kind of hard to do the best I can when I was riding the pine the entire second half.

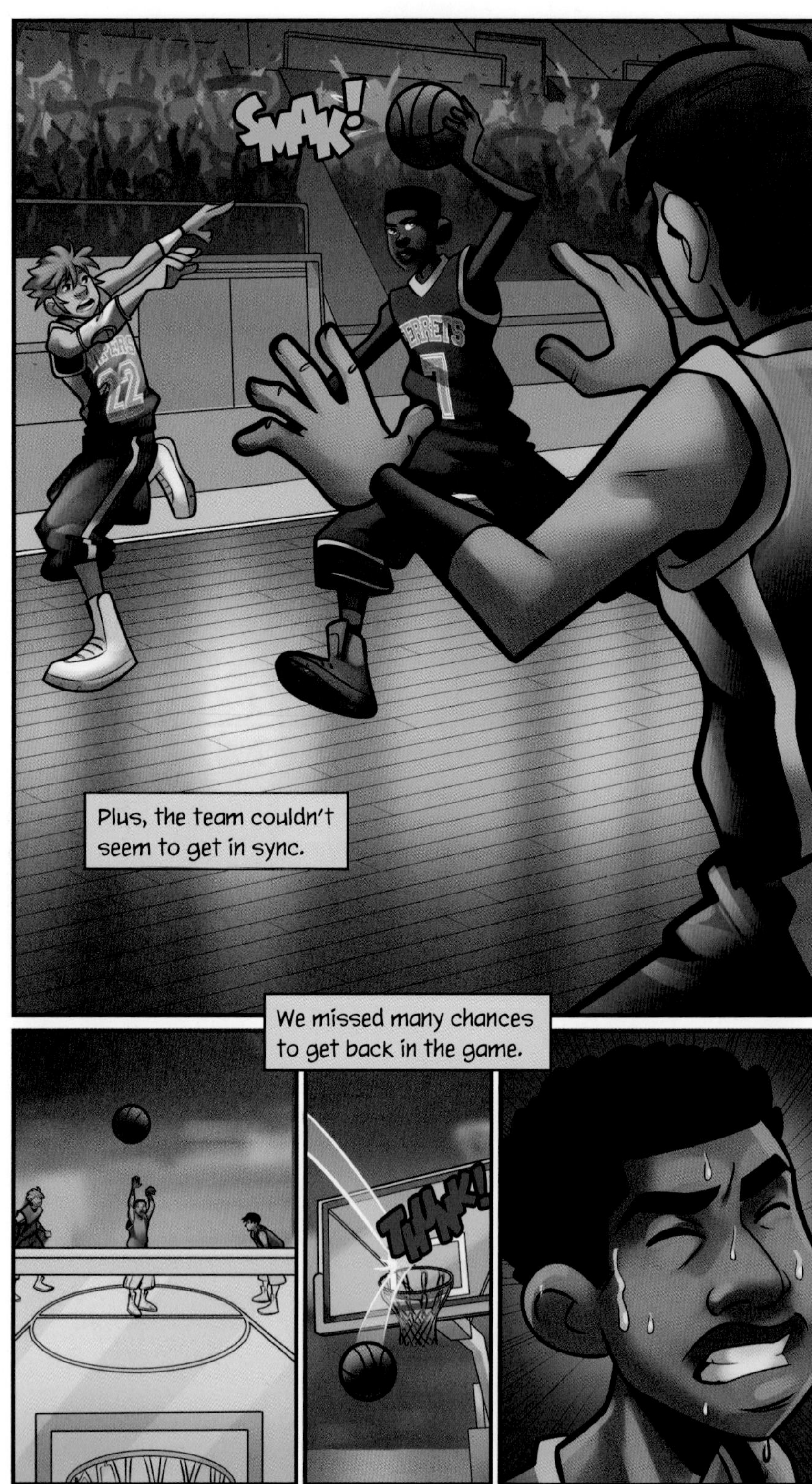
SMAK!
FERRETS
Plus, the team couldn't seem to get in sync.
We missed many chances to get back in the game.
THNK!

SWISH!

. . . I couldn't help but think that this loss was all my fault.

I'd messed up the ingredients for the team. The whole recipe was out of whack. The team wasn't working the way it should.

And it left a bad taste in my mouth.

My luck at home wasn't any better.

I'd suddenly seemed to have forgotten everything gramma taught me about cooking.
THWUMP!

Coach kept me sidelined while my hand healed.

But even after I got back in the game, I still struggled.
KLANG!
Home
Guests
1 2 3 4
bonus
period
bonus
VIPER
15
VIPER
22
Nothing was going right. I couldn't find the right balance.

I had to make a decision.

What was more important to me?

BZZT
BZZT

Abdi

Dood. Wassup? You missed practice.

Yeah, need 2 focus on the cooking audition. No more B-ball, sorry

Abdi
Dood. Wassup? You missed practice.
Yeah, need 2 focus on the cooking audition. No more B-ball, sorry
Can't u do both? Don't understand.

I guess I didn't really understand either.
I just didn't think I could do both.

How's the alfredo sauce taste? Too much garlic?

Mmmmm . . . Nope! It's just right!

But the guys . . . I guess they had other ideas.

DING DONG!

Hank!
It's for
you!

Be right
there!

Okay,
Gracie, I'm
here. So
what's u—
oh.

Hey, man.

Wha . . . what are you guys doing here?

We were just in the neighborhood, thought we'd stop by.
Something smells really good. You gonna invite us in or what?

Uh, if this is about missing practice, I'm sorry, guys. I just can't do it.

I know the game against Freemont is coming up, but I've got to focus on cooking now.

Hank. Dude. You know me. I love basketball more than anything.

But I also love to write. Songs. Poems. Short stories . . . you name it.
V
INK PAWA!

And I like painting miniatures for role-playing games.

Hey.

Sorry about that halftime outburst the other day. You . . . you didn't deserve that.
I'm sorry I made it seem like you had to pick between us and your audition.
It's actually pretty cool what you're doing.

I, uh . . . I love nature photography. Birds in particular.
I've never told anyone, but I really love it.

See? You're not alone. We all have hobbies and passions outside of basketball. But we still love the game too.
You don't need to feel like you have to hide or run away from the team. 
So what do you say?

Fettuccine alfredo?! Oh, man. I haven't had this in forever.

Smells so good.

Mmmph . . . tastes even better.

Because our next game was against the Freemont Leopards. It was one of the toughest teams we'd face all season.

My right hand still stung, but I could manage the pain.

And I knew I could rely on my teammates to back me up.
VIPERS
12

VIPERS
12

SWISH!

We had the right mix of ingredients on the court again. And it felt good.

But like I said. The Leopards were good. Better than any team we'd played yet.
I was still worried about the KidzCook audition too. It was just days away.
Ratatouille
RECIPE
Focaccia
RECIPE
I'm open!
VIPERS
15
But I needed to focus.
If I didn't, I'd spend the game turning over the ball. And that would likely get me a well-deserved spot warming the bench again.

But eventually, the Leopards pulled out in front.

SWISH!

Time out!

I know you're exhausted. You've all played hard and given it your all.

But there's not a lot of time. We've got to score quickly, then try to foul or turn the ball over. Got it?

GOT IT!

Charlie was our best shooter, so we got the ball into his hands.
VIPERS
22

SWISH!
10
12
22
He did exactly what he needed to do. We were down by two.

COUGARS
12
All they needed to do was hold onto the ball. They wanted us to foul them, so they could shoot free throws.

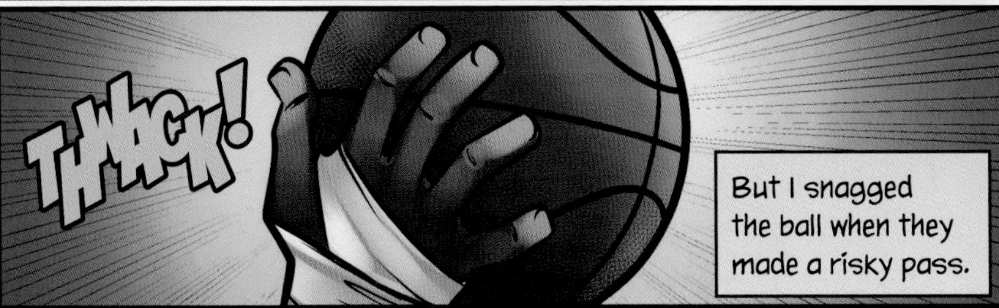
THWACK!
But I snagged the ball when they made a risky pass.

There were less than ten seconds left, and I had a clear path down the court.
00:08
Okay, maybe it wasn't as clear as I thought.
COUGARS
12

So I pulled up at the three-point line. I didn't want to tie the game.

12
14
I wanted to finish it.

BZZZTT!

Yeah.
Nothin' but net.
We won 61-60.
You know, this whole experience taught me a lot about myself.

VIPERS
15
VIPERS
22
34

Kidz COOK
I learned how important is to follow your passions, whatever they might be, and however many you may have.
Follow them with your whole heart.

. . . I wouldn't be here at KidzCook. And I wouldn't be impressing my idol, Brenton Spooner, with my cooking.

No matter how tough the competition might be, I say . . . bring it on!

THE END

MAKE YOUR OWN SPAGHETTI ALLA CARBONARA

Playing your best in any sport requires a lot of energy. Get yourself fueled up for the next big game with this tasty dish you can make yourself.

INGREDIENTS

1 package spaghetti noodles

Salt

4 large eggs

8 ounces (227 grams) freshly grated Parmesan cheese

Fresh ground black pepper, to taste

10 pieces of thick-sliced bacon, coarsely chopped

2 cloves garlic, minced

Fresh chopped parsley, to taste

DIRECTIONS

1. Cook spaghetti in large pot of salted boiling water according to package directions.
2. In a medium bowl, whisk together the eggs with the Parmesan cheese and pepper until well-mixed. Set aside.
3. While spaghetti is cooking, fry chopped bacon in a large skillet over medium heat until brown and slightly crispy.
4. Add minced garlic to the skillet and cook about 1 minute. Remove pan from heat.
5. Use tongs to move cooked spaghetti to the skillet. A little water from the noodles is fine.
6. Pour egg and cheese mixture over the hot noodles and stir quickly until creamy. Keep mixing with the noodles to avoid scrambling the eggs. If sauce is too thick, stir in a little of the starchy pasta water.
7. Serve pasta on plates or in a large bowl. Sprinkle with more Parmesan cheese, pepper, and chopped parsley to taste.

14

Text by Katie Schenkel
Art by Berenice Muñiz
Lettering by Jaymes Reed

THE STARTING LINEUP

NICOLE

KIMBRA AND KYLIE

COACH PAM

Even after packing and saying goodbye to Dad, I couldn't believe I was on my way to the Tracy A. Fremont Girls Basketball Camp.

My school's sports programs only started at junior high.

I didn't have a *real* team of my own, but I had learned basketball by playing pickup games.

And I was the best shooter in the whole neighborhood.

When Dad convinced me to sign up for the big city-wide free throw contest, I never thought I'd win.
FREE THROW CONTEST
But I did.

And I got the grand prize—a full scholarship to a real basketball camp.
TRACY A. FREMONT GIRLS BASKETBALL CAMP
No cell phone, no computers, no distractions. Just four weeks of serious training.

I was going to have a *real* coach and a *real* team and—
Excuse me.
KICK!
KICK!
KICK!

You're shaking my seat.
Sorry. I'm just so excited!

Please stop. I'm trying to read.
Oh.

All right, kids . . .
We're here.

Check in under your assigned team name.
Wait, which team am I on?
Ana Ramirez?

Uh, yes?
I thought I recognized you. The free throw whiz kid herself.
RED COUGARS

Heh, I guess so.
RED COUGARS
I'm Coach Pam. *Your* coach, in fact.

Oh, wow. It's so good to meet you!
I am *really* excited about camp.
RED COUGARS
I'm excited too.
After seeing the contest video, I expect great things from you.

Let's get you signed in. Then you can meet the other Red Cougars.

Hey, Gabby!
Come say hello
to Ana.

It's
you!

Oh, you two
know each
other?
We met on
the bus.
So *you're* the
free throw girl
Coach told me
about, huh?

Uh, yeah.
I am.
I've chosen
Gabby as team
captain. She was
one of my best
players last year.
We nearly got to
the finals.

Hi!!
Ack!

I'm Nicole.
Don't worry about being new. Last summer was my first time at camp, and I had so much fun.
Oh, hello.

Plus Kylie and Kimbra are new, just like you.
Hello!

All right, girls, before you go enjoy the welcome dinner, I want to tell you something.

As a senior staff member, I had the honor of handpicking my players. I think you five will be my best team yet.

The girls and I *did* enjoy the BBQ at the welcome dinner . . .
But soon enough, we found ourselves at the basketball courts.

These girls loved basketball just as much as I did.
And they were *good.*

Nicole was all defense.

The twins were all about speed.
And Gabby . . .

Gabby knew her stuff. The first night, she was already suggesting plays to fit our strengths. And she was a great center. She made tons of rebounds.
No wonder Coach made her captain.

They're all so great.
And Coach Pam picked *me* to be on the team with them.
Wow.

It's awesome our team gets to share a room!
Yeah!
It'll be so much fun!

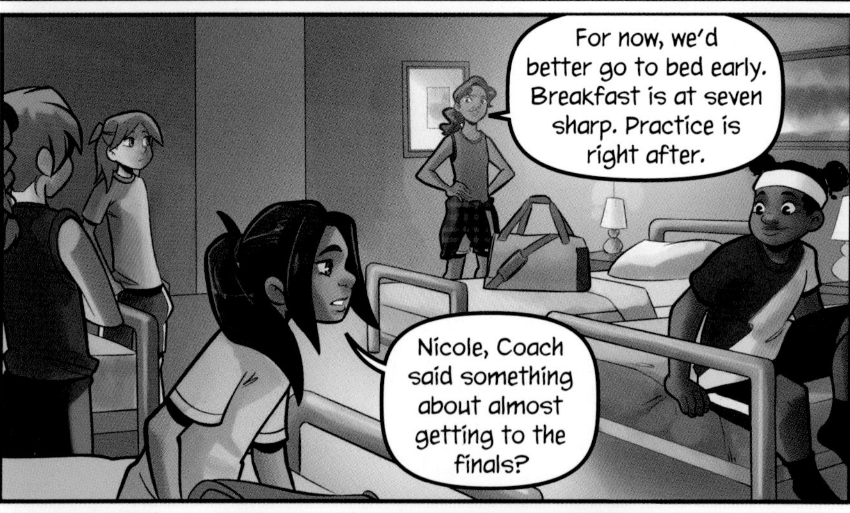
For now, we'd better go to bed early. Breakfast is at seven sharp. Practice is right after.
Nicole, Coach said something about almost getting to the finals?

Oh, that's the tournament finals.
Every year, the teams face off in a big tournament during the last week of camp.

Last year we got to the final four, but—
We didn't win.

But hey, Coach says *this* year's team is the best lineup she's ever had! And we've got a free throw superstar now!

Don't worry, Gabby. With this team? We're going to make it to the finals, and we're going to win.
Guaranteed.

I can't wait until tomorrow.

The next day, we got to work.

COUGARS
4
COUGARS
3
2
COUGA
17

COUGARS
4
COUGARS
14

SWISH!
Nice, Ana!

Coach wasn't kidding about your free throws.
Aw, it was nothing.
COUGARS

Ten in a row isn't *nothing!* Your shots are going to come in handy during the tournament.
COUGARS
14

Wow, so *this* is what it's like to be part of a real team!
All right, time for lunch!
COUGARS
14

Heads up for the newbies.
Every day, practice is going to end with another team joining us for a pickup game.
This gives you all a chance to work together on the court against a real opponent.
COUGARS
17
2
3

Now, as we prepare for the tournament, I want you all to use zone tactics in our defense during these games.
Zone tactics?
COUGARS
17
2
COUGARS 14
3

Everyone is familiar with 2-3 zone defense, right?
Yes, Coach!
Uh . . . yes, Coach.
COUGARS

So for today, I want Nicole to—
Why did I say I knew what she's talking about?!

But everyone already thinks I'm a great player.
If I ask Coach now, the girls will think I'm a phony.
What am I going to do?

Everyone know their positions?
Yes, Coach!

Then let's go beat the Blue Bulldogs!
Maybe I can figure it out on the court.

COUGARS
17
21
COUGARS
4
Despite my nerves, we started off strong.

21

COUGARS
14

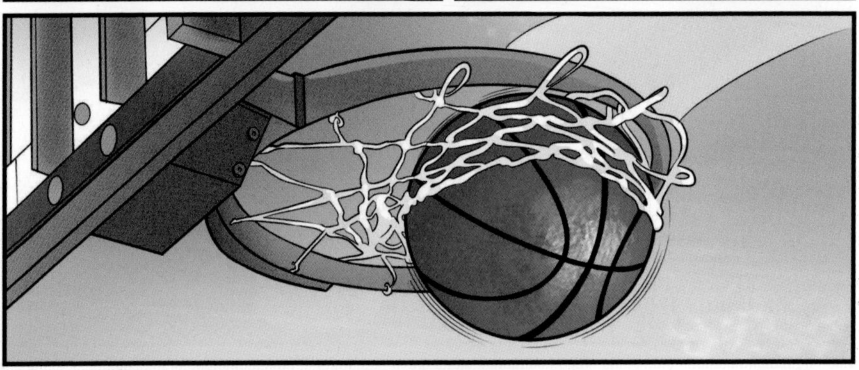

YES!
Way to go, girls!
Now defense, like we talked about!

Wait, where am I supposed to go?

Am I supposed to focus on one of the Bulldogs? Or–
Look out!

Oomf!

SWOOP!

Ow.
What was that?!

Let's go!

Where was I supposed to go back there? Do I need to stay in one spot on offense too? What do I do?

Ana! Rebound!

Argh!

BULLDOGS
11

Yeah, Brielle!
Good job!

A while later.
Woo!
A twelve to four win! Not bad for our first game, girls.
Yeah!

OK, team, huddle up.

A loss is always frustrating.
You all did great during practice, but I saw some sloppy work in the game.

Kimbra, you need to remember to pivot.
OUGARS

Gabby, your shooting choices need work.
OUGARS

And Ana . . .
Uh . . . yes, Coach?

Work on that zone defense.
Yes, Coach.

At dinner.

That was embarrassing.

Well, it was just a practice game. Everyone has bad days.

It did take Kimbra and me a while to get used to our school team.
Exactly. We have time to work out the problems. We'll be ready by the tournament.

Right, Ana?

Right. Definitely.

SLOPPY WORK
SLOPPY WORK
SLOPPY WORK
SLOPPY WORK

The next day.
Gotta work hard.

Gotta keep going.
Can't let the team down.

Good job, girls! I'm liking your drive today.

Um, Coach? About the defense . . .

Yes, Ana?

Uh . . .

Never mind.

I tried my best, but I didn't know where to go.

We got a few points at first . . .

SWISH!

The Red Cougars weren't working together.
COUGARS
14

Things just kept getting worse.
BONK!

And worse.
TORNADOS
COUGARS

And worse.

OK, so that wasn't great.

"Wasn't great"?
We've had two terrible games in a row. The twins kept traveling and I couldn't make a shot and Ana crashed into you! Again!

Yeah . . . it was a mess.
What are we doing wrong?
Whatever is going on, we've got to do better or we have no shot of winning the tournament.

Team, can I have a word?

I know we did bad today, Coach. I was just telling the team—

We'll discuss game play in the morning. That's not what I want to talk about.

We can't play well if we're so tense!
Maybe we should just chill out tonight and do something fun.
That's a great idea, Kylie!
Ana, do you have any ideas for—

Ana?

WOMP!

I'm failing.
My first week on a real basketball team and it's all gone wrong.
And without my phone or the internet, I can't even look up how I'm messing up.

All the other girls are so good.
They know what they're doing. They know what zone defense is.

If I say something, they'll think I'm weak.
Or what if Coach tries to explain and I still can't get it? Will the girls even want me on the team?

We missed you at dinner.

I wasn't feeling well.
Oh no! I hope you're not getting sick.

If you'd be up for it, the team and a few other girls are getting out the karaoke machine. It's a camp tradition to do karaoke at least once.
What do you say?
UGAR
4

I don't know...
Please? We really want our whole team there. You don't have to sing. Gabby isn't planning to either.

Plus, you *did* miss dinner and there are snacks downstairs. Eating might help you feel better even if the singing doesn't.
UGAR
4
Well, OK. But I'll probably just watch.

And if you don't know . . .
Then you gotta goooooo!

♪ And if you don't know . . .

♫ Then ♫ you gotta gooooooo! ♪

Awesome job!

Wooo!

Why, thank you.

Ha ha!

Me too.

Only fifteen minutes until lights out. We have time for one last song.
I'll take a shot at it.

You? Really?
Sure. I can't let you girls have all the fun.

I'm so happy you're feeling better. I couldn't have rocked that duet without you!
Ha ha!

When we win the tournament, you and I are definitely singing a victory song.

Oh. Sure.

The girls tonight were so great to me. It's like we're real friends.
I can't let them down.

All right, no more feeling sorry for myself.
First thing in the morning, I'm going to figure out zone defense.

On my own.

First thing in the morning.

CREEAK
Huh?

Hmm.

OK, I definitely remember Coach telling me to go here.

Or maybe I'm supposed to be over there?

I am so in over my head.
Hey.

Gabby!
I was hoping you'd be here. I wanted your advice.

You want advice. From *me*?
Yeah.

You see, I've always had trouble with my distance shooting. And you're so good at it . . .

Could you give me some pointers?
Umm . . .

Sure. I can help with that.

A while later.
BONK!

Dang it!
That one was so close. Try again.

I was keeping my wrists loose, like you said.
I can tell. Your form is already looking better.

You know, it was my fault. Losing the final game last year.
I had the last shot and I missed. I was never great at shooting, but since then I've just gotten worse.

I think half the time my problem is getting stuck in my own head.

Does that make sense?
Yeah.
That makes a *lot* of sense.

This time, relax your shoulders.
Keep your eye on the rim as you're taking your shot.

Hoo.

SWISH!

There you go!
Oh my gosh!
CLAP!

Thanks, Ana. This helped a ton.
Oh, it's no big deal.

You're so good, I still can't believe you wanted *my* help.

Teammates are there to support each other. There's no shame in asking for help.

Well, I guess we better get to breakfast—
Hey, Gabby?

I could use some help understanding zone defense.
But only if you have the time.

Of course I have time.

So if I'm this one here . . .
Then you're the X just to the right of the basket. Nicole is on the other side, and the twins are in front.
You want to cover your area of the court.
But those are just our starting points. Depending on what the other team does, we shift our positions.
So I don't have to stay still?
Nope! It's more about making sure our defense covers the most ground.
Ha ha.
I feel so silly. I could have learned all this days ago.

Instead, I made myself sick with nerves.
I didn't want to seem like . . .
. . .the weak link.

Hey. No one knows everything right away.

Just tell Coach or the rest of us if you need help.
None of us are mind readers.

Except maybe the twins, but only with each other.
Ha ha!

Morning practice.
So you see, I need more time to understand zone defense.
If that's OK.
Hmm. Thanks for coming to me, Ana.

Gather round, girls. Before we get to work this morning, I want to say something.
We've been covering a lot of skills very quickly. I don't want anyone to feel lost as we play.

I'm here to help. If anyone is confused about anything, just ask me about it.
Coach?

I haven't gotten the hang of pivots. I think that's why I keep getting called for traveling.
COUGARS

Thank you for speaking up, Kimbra. We'll work on that this morning.
We'll also go over zone defense again.

Then we'll start planning out offensive plays for the tournament.
It's only two weeks away, but I know we'll be ready.
Now let's get started!
COUGARS
14

I can't believe it. I really wasn't the only one struggling.
Told you.

Maybe I *can* do this!

That afternoon.

Come on, Ana. You've got this.
Remember what Gabby said. Defend your space. Look for opportunity.

This is it.

COUGARS
14

Go, go, go!

FWISH!

That's how it's done!
Yeah!
Way to go, Ana!

By the time the tournament started, we were a well-oiled machine.

Our zone defense held off our opponents . . .

And I racked up the points.

We took the tournament by storm!

The finals against the Blue Bulldogs—the opponents from our very first practice.

These girls were just as tough as the first time we faced them . . .
90
COUGARS

But we were giving our all.

COUGAR
4
42

Throughout the game . . .

It was neck and neck.

Until . . .

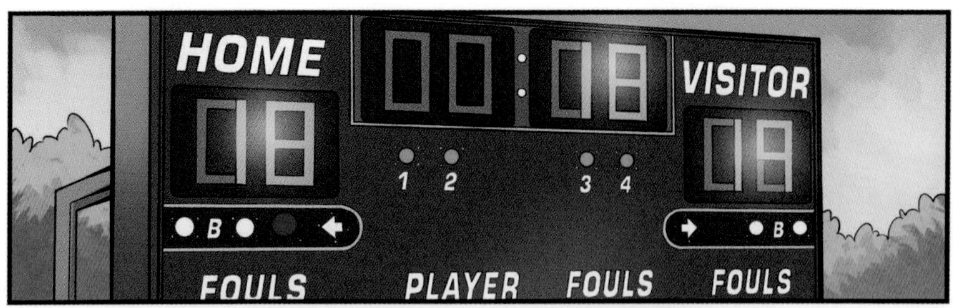
HOME
VISITOR
FOULS
PLAYER
FOULS
FOULS

We need another basket, but I can't make the shot!

Wait! Gabby is open!

COUGARS 17

Come on, Gabby!

SWISH!

Cougars win the tournament!
Way to go, Gabby!
Woo!

I would like to make a toast.
GO COUGAR
PIZZA
PIZZA

To the best team I've ever coached at the Tracy A. Fremont Girls Basketball Camp.

To the Cougars!
COUGARS!
COUGARS!

And to Gabby and that amazing last second shot!
Well, I couldn't have done it without Ana's help.

Really, your shooting lesson helped me a ton. Thanks.
Hey, maybe we should get out the karaoke machine to celebrate.
Good idea. Heck, I'll even do the first number.

HA! HA! HA! HA! HA! HA! HA! HA!

The next day.
Oh, the last day of camp always makes me cry.

Sorry to break this up, but Ana and Gabby's bus is here.
I gave you all my number, right?

Can't wait to see you two next year.
Bye!

Want to share seats this time?
That sounds great, Captain.

Pretty cool, huh? Your first summer here, and you're already a camp champ.

Ha, yeah.

CHAMPION
Being camp champ is pretty great.

But I knew what I would really remember about that summer.
CHAMPION
SEASON

THE HISTORY OF WOMEN'S BASKETBALL

1891 - Basketball is invented by Canadian American and physical education teacher James Naismith.

1892 - The first women's basketball game is organized by Smith College's Senda Berenson. She changes Naismith's rules to emphasize cooperation and zone playing.

1914 - The American Olympic Committee officially declares it is against women taking part in Olympic competitions.

1926 - The Amateur Athletic Union (AAU) holds the first national basketball tournament for women.

1936 - A women's basketball team called the All-American Red Heads starts traveling across the United States. They compete (and often win) against men's teams. They are a huge hit with crowds.

1955 - The second Pan American Games includes women's basketball as an event.

1976 - Women's basketball becomes an official Olympic sport.

1982 - The first National Collegiate Athletic Association (NCAA) women's basketball tournament is held.

1996 - The National Basketball Association (NBA) establishes the Women's National Basketball Association (WNBA). The league starts with eight teams.

2016 - The WNBA celebrates its 20th season and is now made up of twelve teams.

BASKETBALL LEGENDS

CHERYL MILLER

Playing in the 1980s, Cheryl Miller was a basketball superstar well before the WNBA was formed. A gold medal Olympian, NCAA champion, and *Sports Illustrated*'s 1985 National Player of the Year, Miller made America think differently about female basketball players.

PAT SUMMITT

University of Tennessee head coach Pat Summitt led her women's team to eight NCAA championships. In her 48-year career from 1974 to 2012, she was the first NCAA coach in any sport to win over 1,000 games with a single team.

CANDACE PARKER

When she was drafted into the WNBA by the Los Angeles Sparks in 2008, Candace Parker made fans take notice. That year, she won both the Rookie of the Year and Most Valuable Player awards. Since then she's become a WNBA champion as well as a two-time Olympic gold medalist. She is one of the WNBA's best players.

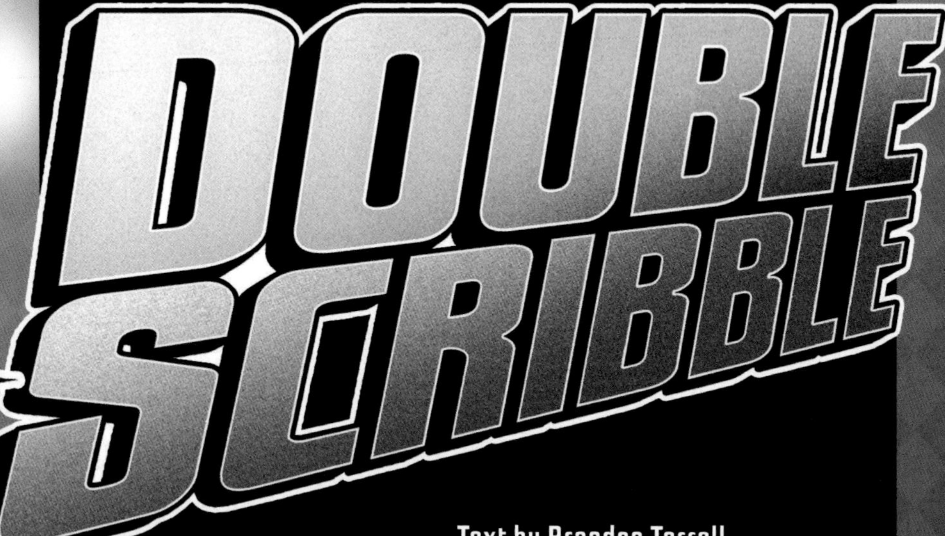

Text by Brandon Terrell

Art by Aburtov

Lettering by Jaymes Reed

STARTING LINEUP

F
8
REGGIE CARLSON

LAILA AHMADI

COACH BANNER

Last season, my team, the Martinsville Cougars, were state champs.
33
We won the big game with a bit of last-second heroics by yours truly.
GO HARD
COUGARS
23
Drawing this out in my sketchbook was my dad's idea. I'll get to that later.
My name is Diego, but I earned my nickname after the championship game. That's when the team started calling me —
"CLUTCH!"

Here's how it happened.
We were down by one point with only a few seconds left on the clock.
00:10
I got the ball to our best shooter, Malcolm Downs.
00:08

Malcolm was double-teamed.

There was no way he was putting up the shot.

I didn't have time to think. Once I got the ball, I needed to take the shot.

Nothin' but nylon.
When the buzzer sounded, the Cougars were champs.
That was last season, though. *This* season has been a different story . . .
Diego! Time for school!

One week earlier . . .
PEP RALLY TODAY
MARTINSVILLE MIDDLE SCHOOL
Good afternoon, Cougar Country!
Today's pep rally to kick off the Cougars basketball season starts in just ten minutes!
So let me hear you
ROOOOOOOAR!
Hey, Clutch! Can't wait for the game tonight!
Bring us home another trophy!

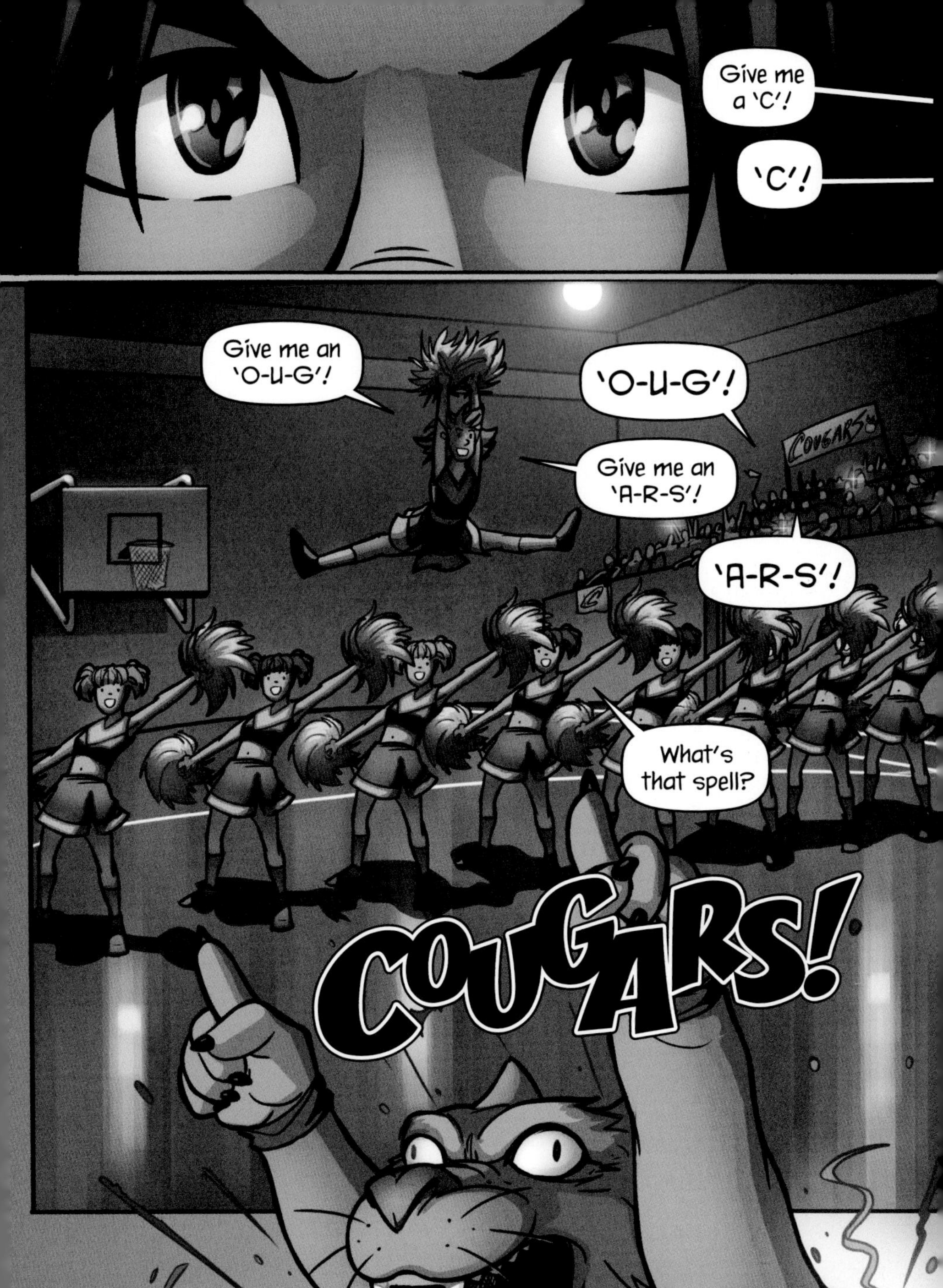

Give me a 'C'!
'C'!
Give me an 'O-U-G'!
'O-U-G'!
Give me an 'A-R-S'!
'A-R-S'!
What's that spell?
COUGARS!
ROOOOOOAR!

Greetings, Martinsville Middle School Fighting Cougars!
Tonight marks the start of another season . . .
Thank you all for your amazing support of our *championship* boys basketball team.
And with it, another chance at the state tournament . . .
. . . where we'll hopefully bring home this trophy's identical twin!
Now, a word from Coach Banner.

Thank you, Principal Cline. And thank *you*, Cougar Country!
CLUTCH
Let's pack the stands tonight when we tame the Mustangs!
Wooo!
Yeah!
Go Cougars!
There's five players on the court all the time, giving it their all.
We play as a team, and we win and lose as a team.

But that doesn't mean we shouldn't recognize last season's championship game MVP.
Let's bring him up. You know him, you love him . . .
3

Diego 'Clutch' Rivera!
Wooo!
I love you, Clutch!
ROOOOOOAR!
Yeah, things were looking up after that pep rally.
I felt like I was on top of the world . . .

But that was
before the game . . .
The Mustangs were
a tough team.
We gave them everything we had.

SWISH
But they quickly matched whatever points we scored.

ROOOOOOAR!
The game kept going back and forth. We'd score, then they'd put up points too.
COUGARS 46
GUEST 49
We were down by three, with time running out.

Make the shot,
then full court press!
Foul when you can!
Malcolm nailed a big
jump shot. We were
down by just one point!
And then, with just a
few seconds left . . .

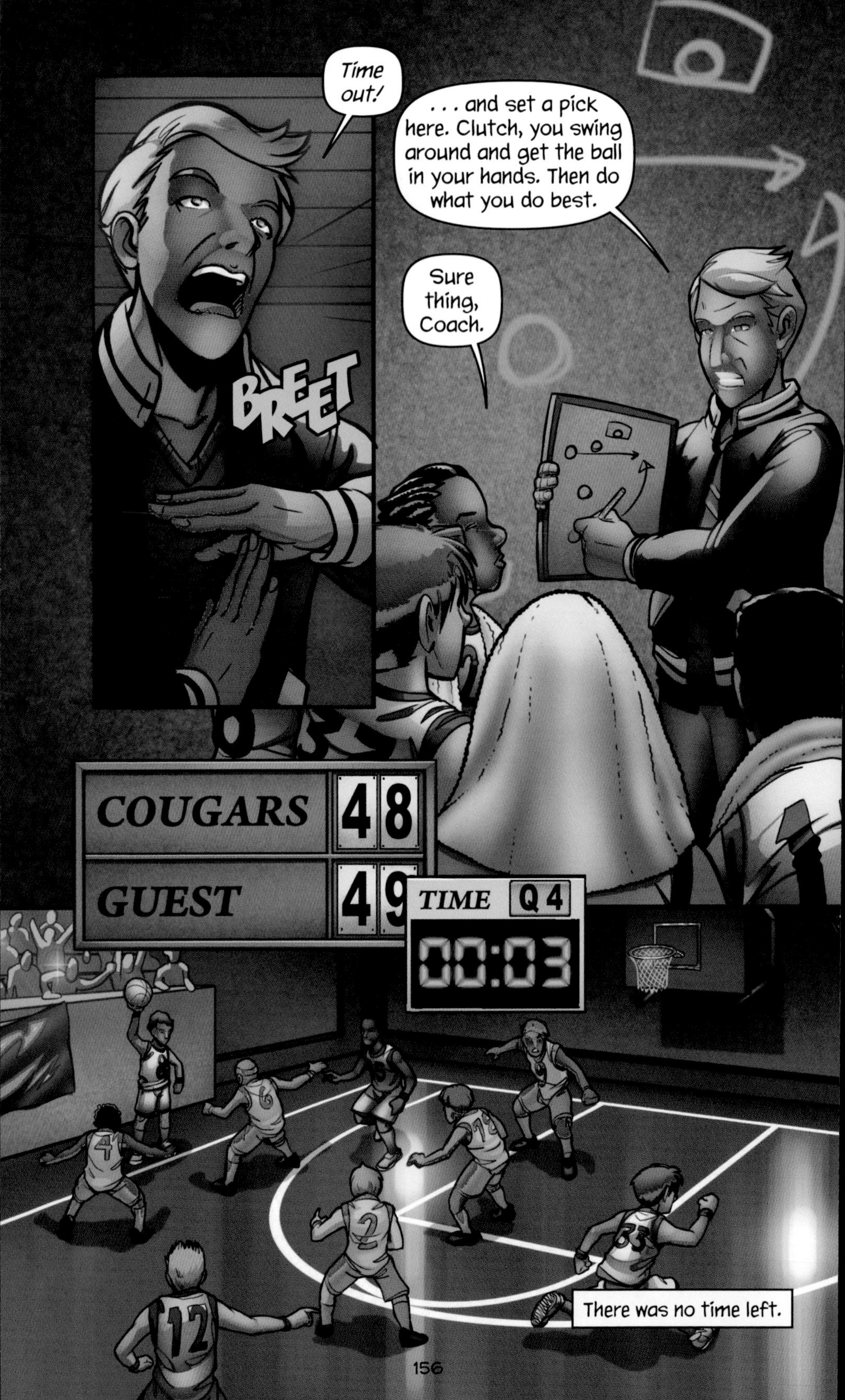
Time out!
BREET
. . . and set a pick here. Clutch, you swing around and get the ball in your hands. Then do what you do best.
Sure thing, Coach.
COUGARS 48
GUEST 49
TIME Q4
00:03
There was no time left.

Clutch! Clutch! Clutch!
Clutch! Clutch! Clu—

BRRRZZZZT
CLANK
I missed . . .

I missed.
Nice try, Clutch.

Every time I closed my eyes that night, I saw the shot.
2:16 AM
Yeah, it was just one miss. Just one game.
It shouldn't be a big deal.
But it was.
02:17 AM
CLICK

I had to make sure it was a fluke . . .
. . . that I was still the guy who sank that buzzer-beating hook shot last season.
THUNK

Grrrr!
THUNK
This is ridiculous!
You know the whole neighborhood can hear you, right?
Oh. Uh, sorry Laila.
Did I, uh, wake you up?

What do you think?
So are you "sleep-hooping" or something?
You must not have been at the game tonight.
Nope. Had better things to do.

I missed the game-winning shot.
So?
So?! I have a reputation to keep. The team looks up to me.
THUNK
And I let them down!

CRASH
Whoa . . . Diego? What are you doing out here, pal?
It's after 2 a.m.
CLANG
Nothing.
Evenin', Laila.
Everything okay?
Well, actually . . .

SSSZZZZL
POP
♫
Hunngg.
Welcome back to the land of the living. Have a seat. Eat some grub.
What's this?

It's a sketchbook.
Like a diary?
Well, kind of. Think of it as a way to draw what you're feeling.
I used to have one just like it at your age. Whenever I got upset or angry, I'd draw out how I was feeling.
CRUNCH
It'll help. I promise.
Huh . . . m'kay.
Told you I'd get back to telling you about my sketchbook.

Hey!
Hey.
You're looking quite zombie-like today. When did you wind up falling asleep?
I don't wanna talk about it.
. . . not gonna do that every game, is he?
Man, I *hope* not.

It's okay, I'm not hungry anymore.

THUNK

SPLAT

I wish that missing the trash with my uneaten lunch was the last shot I missed . . .

. . . But it wasn't.
The following game, I picked up right where I left off.
I couldn't concentrate. All I could think was, "Diego! Don't miss!"
WHACK
I mean, I'm supposed to be *Clutch*.

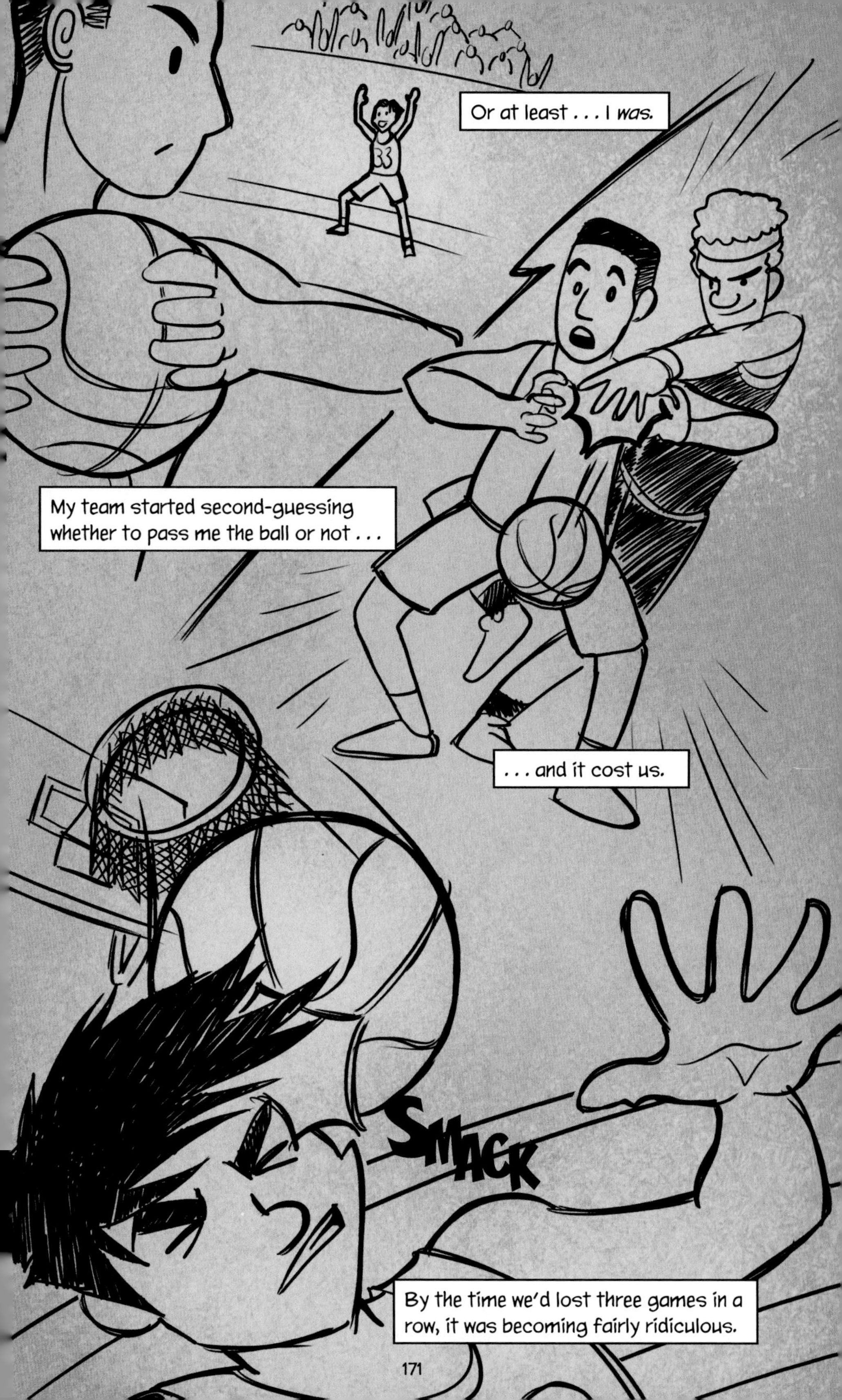
Or at least . . . I *was.*
My team started second-guessing whether to pass me the ball or not . . .
. . . and it cost us.
SMACK
By the time we'd lost three games in a row, it was becoming fairly ridiculous.

Clutch? He's more like *Clank.*
Ha!
Heh. Clank. Good one.
It turned out I had earned a new nickname.
I tried hard not to let it affect me. But it did.

I was struggling both on *and* off the court.
blah, blah, . . . ~~~ ~~~~~ ~~~~
blah, blah, blah, . . . ~~~ ~~~~~ ~~~~~~~
CLANK
CLANK
It was the most frustrating feeling in the world.

All right, Cougars, pay attention.
SNAP!
NSVILLE
GUARS
We've got a big game coming up, probably the biggest of the season.
The Platteville Pythons.
I know we've had a rough start to the season . . .

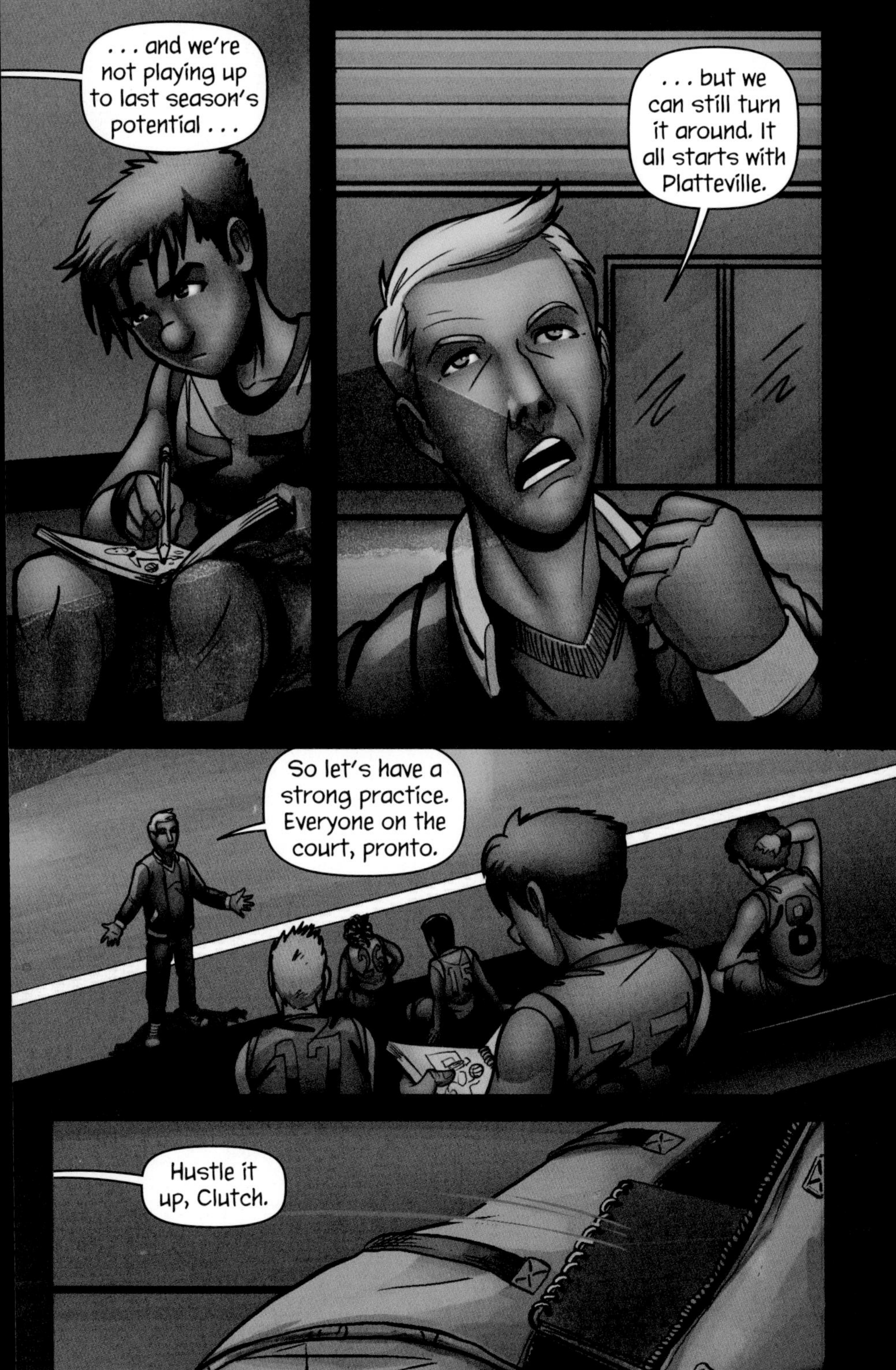
. . . and we're not playing up to last season's potential . . .
. . . but we can still turn it around. It all starts with Platteville.
So let's have a strong practice. Everyone on the court, pronto.
Hustle it up, Clutch.

Yeah, let's go, Clank.
Yeah, I heard him. But I was determined not to let it go to my head.
My head, however, had different ideas.

CLANK
Great shot, Clank!
That's it. I'm outta here!
Dude, come on. It was a joke!
Diego!

No one came to check on me. I didn't care.
I stayed out of sight until practice was over . . .
. . . until I knew the rest of the team was gone.
It wasn't until I was getting dressed that I realized . . .
Where is it?!
Where's my sketchbook?! It must still be in the gym.
Hey, Diego.
Looking for this?
Oh, thank goodness. You found it.

I'm fine.

Wow, *that's* believable.

SNATCH

See, this is why I've never been to a basketball game.
Or . . . any sporting event, come to think of it.
You guys put too much pressure on yourselves.
I thought basketball was supposed to be fun, Diego.
So come on, let's have some fun.
WHUMP

Whatcha got, Clutch? Come at me. Bring it, bro.
Pfft! Your trash talking is terrible.
Well, so's your hook shot.
Ha! Better. Also, ouch.
No! Ahh!
CLANK

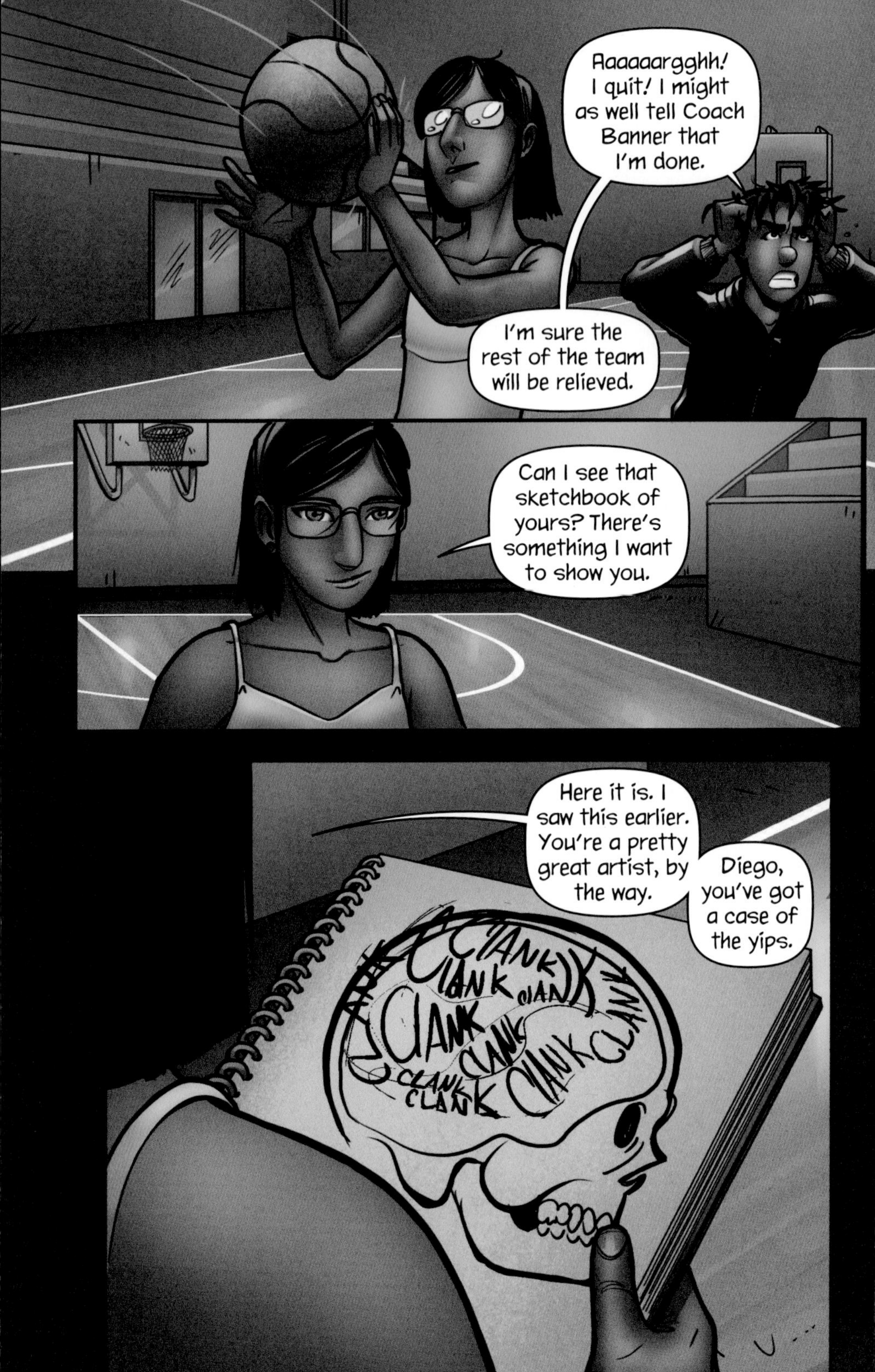
Aaaaaargghh! I quit! I might as well tell Coach Banner that I'm done.
I'm sure the rest of the team will be relieved.
Can I see that sketchbook of yours? There's something I want to show you.
Here it is. I saw this earlier. You're a pretty great artist, by the way.
Diego, you've got a case of the yips.
CLANK
CLANK
CLANK
CLANK
CLANK
CLANK
CLANK
CLANK
CLANK
CLANK

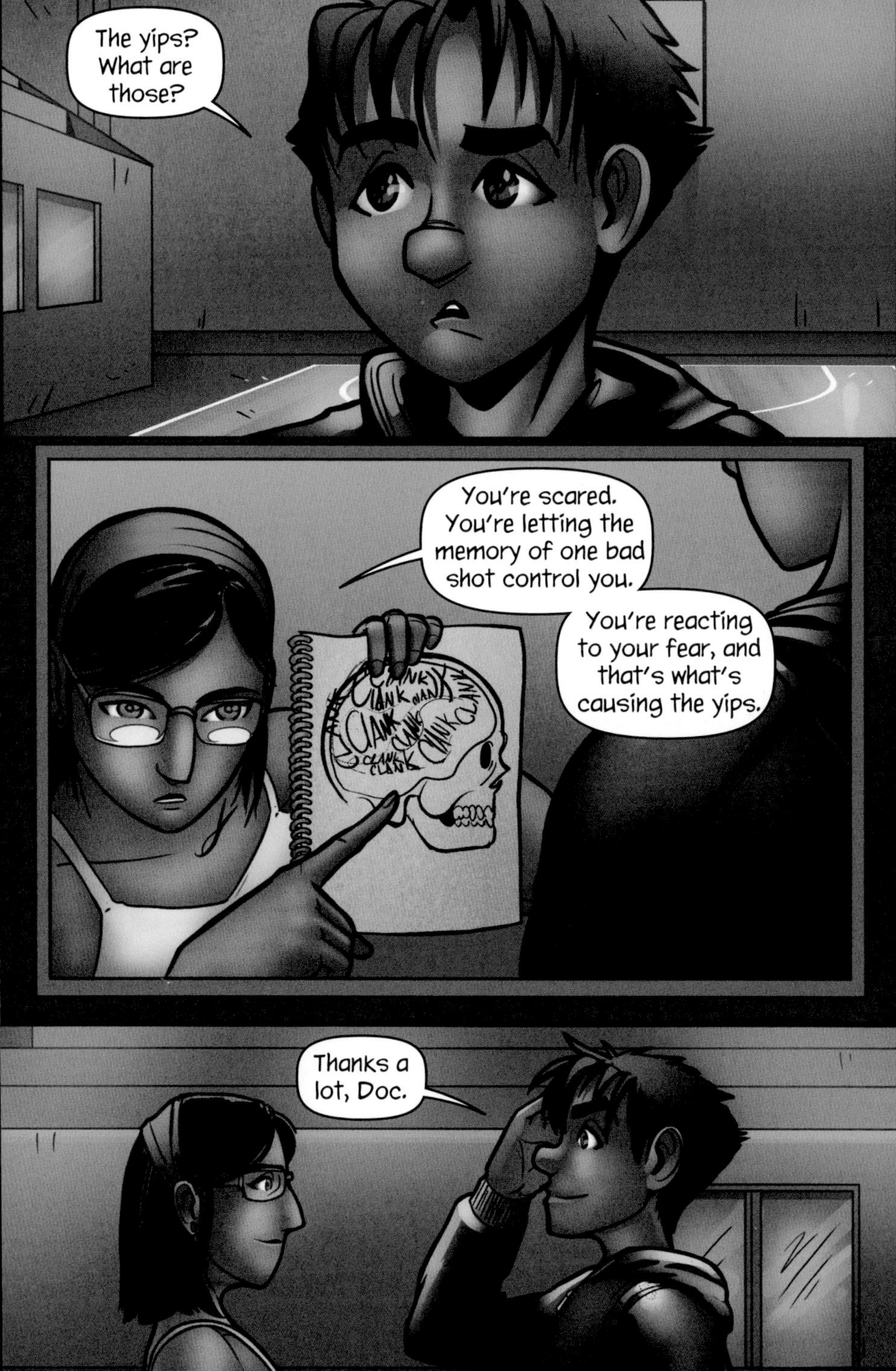
The yips? What are those?
You're scared. You're letting the memory of one bad shot control you.
You're reacting to your fear, and that's what's causing the yips.
Thanks a lot, Doc.

You need to play like you don't care about winning a trophy, Diego.
Have fun, and stop putting so much pressure on yourself.
SWISH
See. Told ya.
Huh.

This is it,
Cougars.
This is our
moment to turn
the whole season
around.

I know we've had a few tough losses, but we can change that today.
Let's go scare those Pythons out of Cougar Country!
Coach's speech was pretty good, but . . .
HiSS!
PYTHO
. . . the other team didn't look very scared.
In fact, their coach looked downright terrifying.

I couldn't let my fears get in my head, though.
Not if I was going to conquer my 'yips.'
BREET
I won the tip, and we were off to a good start.
A few dribbles and a quick shot later . . .

. . . we were the first on the board.
Come on! Tough defense out there!
I had a feeling it was going to be the easiest two points we scored all game.
The Pythons were speedy and efficient. Before we knew it, they changed the whole dynamic of the game.

Shoot it!
Take the shot, Clutch!
Unfortunately, the Pythons got into my head . . .
. . . my fear and self-doubt had crept back in.
THWACK

Dude, you were wide open.
Why didn't you take the shot?
Huh?
Laila? At a basketball game?
Remember, have FUN!
At least I think that was what she said. I'm kind of terrible at reading lips.

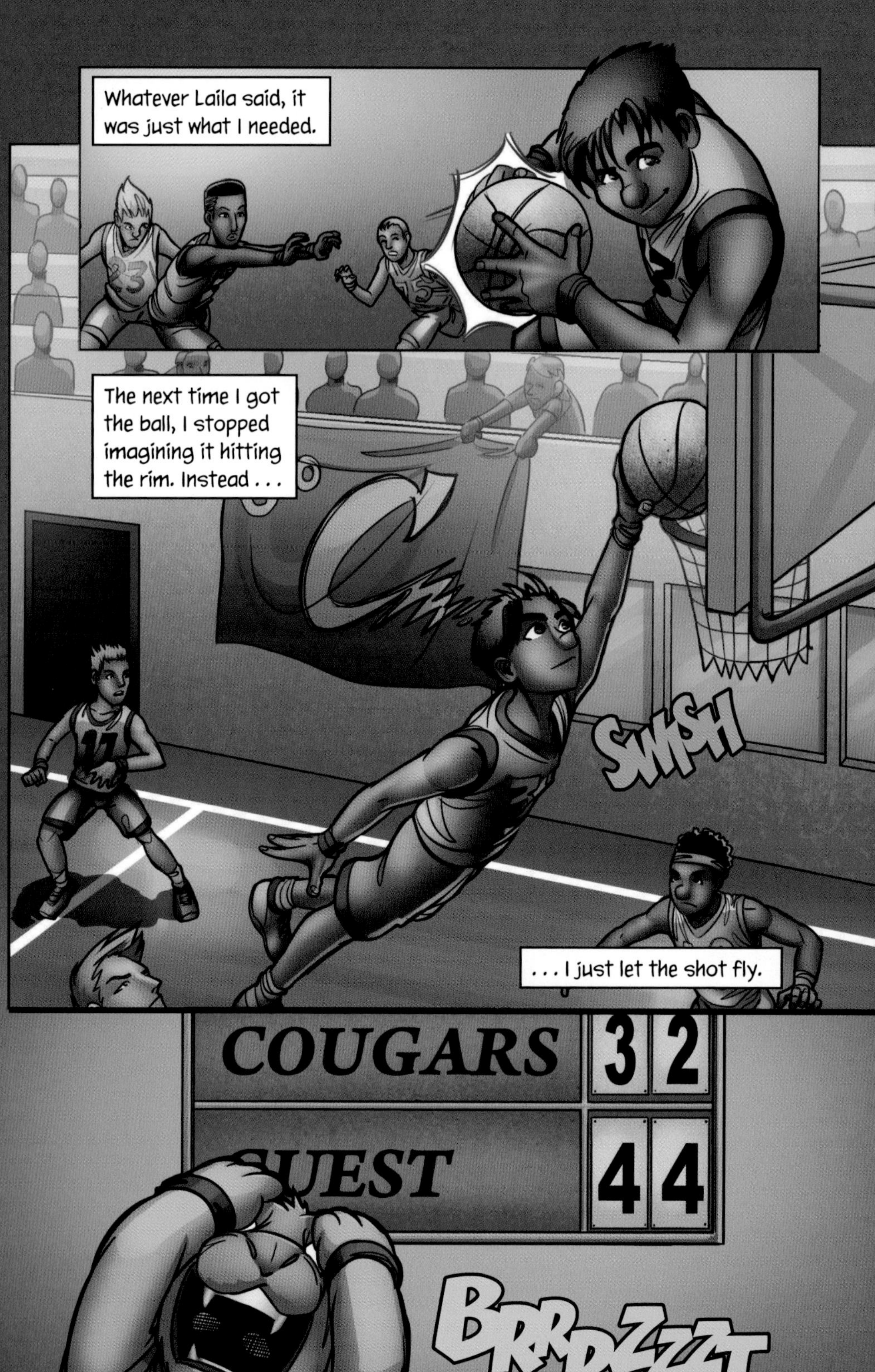
Whatever Laila said, it was just what I needed.
The next time I got the ball, I stopped imagining it hitting the rim. Instead . . .
SWISH
. . . I just let the shot fly.
COUGARS 32
UEST 44
BRRRZZZT

All right, boys. I know we're down, but we're not out. Not by a long shot.
What we're missing out there . . . well, it's —
— heart. We're missing heart. We're playing like we're expecting to lose, and we're not having fun.

Basketball is a game. Yeah, it can be frustrating sometimes . . .
But man, it's a lot of fun.

In the second half, it was like I could *see* the tension slip out of us.
Our feet were lighter, our moves faster. We were in "the zone" . . .
. . . and we stayed there.
Nice hook shot, Clutch.
Thanks.
With ten seconds to go, we had the ball . . .
COUGARS 48
GUEST 49
. . . and one last shot.
My teammates didn't hesitate to give me the ball.
00:06
Clutch!

00:03
THUMP
00:00
BRRRZZZZT
The ball came out of my hand just as the buzzer blared through the gym.
17
I missed . . .
RATTLE
THUNK
BREET
But then . . .

Foul!
Number 23,
green!
Two free
throws!
The first free throw,
I was too caught up in
the moment to worry.
I swear the ball sat
on that rim for an
eternity before . . .

SWISH
Tie game, man. You sink this one, we win.
No pressure, Clutch.
Yeah — no pressure.

It was time to face my fears one last time. I could almost feel them taunting me. But I couldn't let them get to me.

I just needed to take a deep breath . . .

. . . and erase them all.

Leaving nothing but a blank page.

33

Besides, it wasn't a big deal. It was just one shot . . . one game . . .

. . . one point.
SWISH
So yeah, let's see. We beat the Pythons . . .
I conquered my mental block . . .

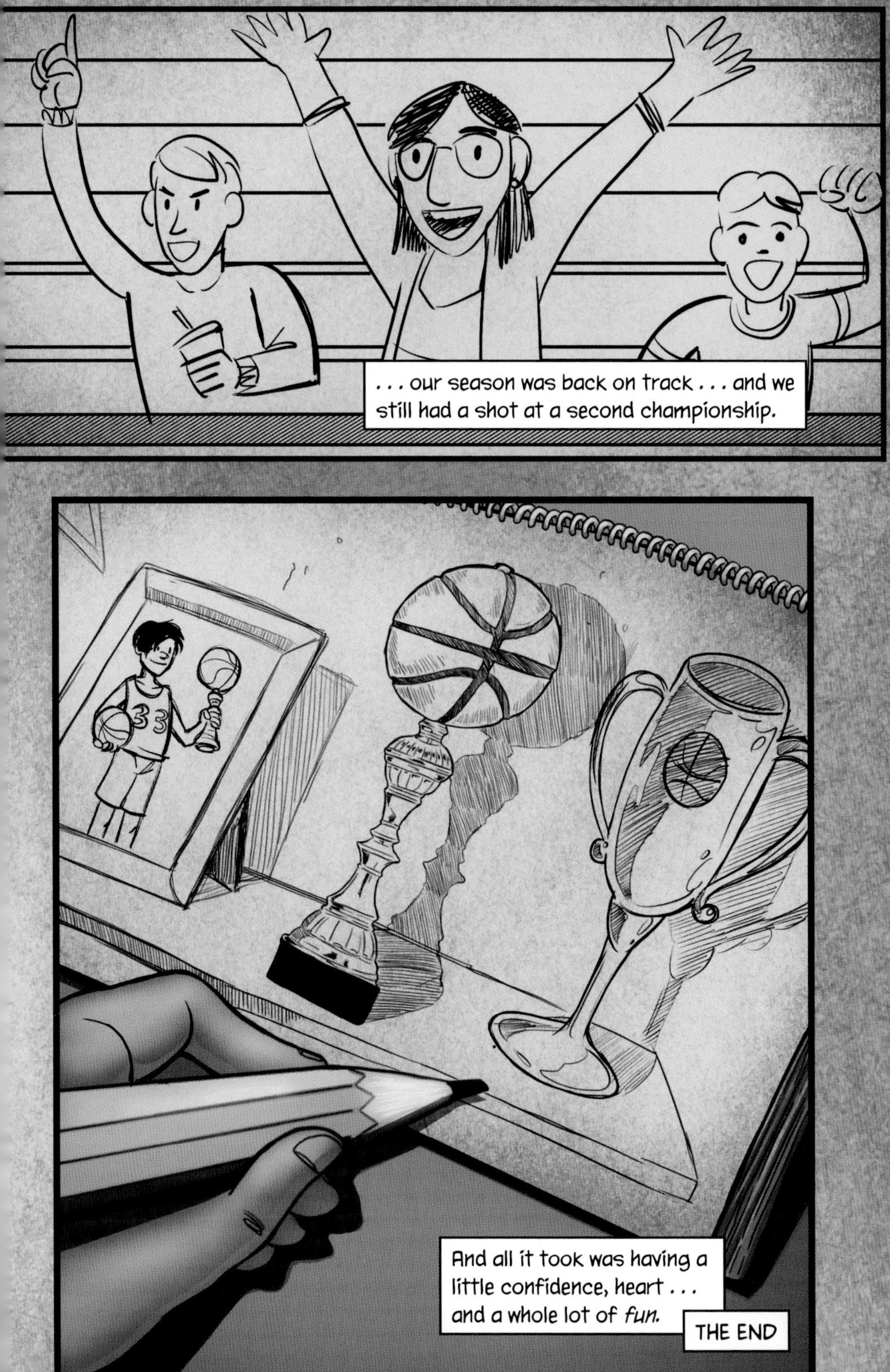

And all it took was having a little confidence, heart . . . and a whole lot of *fun.*

THE END

FUN BASKETBALL FACTS

1. Dr. James Naismith invented the game of basketball in 1891. He created it for athletes at his school in Springfield, Massachusetts who were bored in the winter. Each team had nine players. To score points, the players threw a soccer ball into peach baskets hung from the gym balcony.

2. Basketball was introduced as an Olympic sport at the 1936 Summer Games held in Berlin, Germany.

3. The National Basketball Association (NBA) was formed in 1946, but was originally called the Basketball Association of America. The league's first official game was played on November 1, 1946, between the Toronto Huskies and the New York Knickerbockers.

4. Philadelphia center Wilt Chamberlain scored a record 100 points in a single game on March 2, 1962.

5. Kareem Abdul Jabbar played for 20 seasons in the NBA. He holds the record for the most career points scored with 38,387.

6. The Boston Celtics and the Los Angeles Lakers are tied for the most championships. Each team has won 17 NBA titles.

BASKETBALL TERMS TO KNOW

dribble — to use one hand to repeatedly bounce the ball off the floor; players must dribble the ball as they move up and down the court

fast break — a quick offensive drive to the basket, attempting to beat the defense to the other end of the court

foul — a violation of the rules, usually involving illegal contact with an opposing player

free throw — also known as a foul shot, free throws are awarded after a player is fouled by an opposing player; free throw shots are made from the foul line and are worth one point each

jump ball — a method of putting a basketball into play; the referee throws the ball into the air between two players, who jump up and try to direct it to one of their teammates

jump shot — a shot made while jumping and releasing the ball at the peak of your jump

layup — a shot made from very close to the basket, usually by bouncing the ball off the backboard

pick — to block an opposing player so a teammate can make a shot or receive a pass in open space

rebound — to catch the basketball after a shot has been missed

three-pointer — a successful shot from outside the designated arc of the three-point line on a basketball court

turnover — when a player loses possession of the ball to the opposing team

AUTHORS

Brandon Terrell (B.1978 – D.2021) Brandon was a passionate reader, Star Wars enthusiast, amazing father, son, uncle, friend, and devoted husband. He worked as an assistant director and producer on numerous independent films and commercial productions as well as a writer for the *Choo Choo Bob Show*. Brandon received his undergraduate degree from the Minneapolis College of Art and Design and his Master of Fine Arts in Writing for Children and Young Adults from Hamline University in St. Paul, MN. Brandon was a talented storyteller, authoring more than 100 books for children in his career. In Brandon's memory, consider picking up a Stephen King novel or a comic book, re-watching *The Mandalorian*, reading an old Hardy Boys adventure, and saving an open seat for the next Star Wars movie.

Katie Schenkel is a comic writer best known for the critically acclaimed, Eisner Award-nominated graphic novel *The Cardboard Kingdom*. She especially loves to write about girls' friendships and their perspectives on the world around them. Katie was a competitive swimmer for many years, so writing *Swim Team Trouble* was very special for her. Midwest to her core, Katie lives in Chicago with her partner, Madison.

ARTISTS

Berenice Muñiz is a graphic designer and illustrator from Monterrey, Mexico. She has done work for publicity agencies, art exhibitions, and even created her own webcomic. These days, Berenice is devoted to illustrating comics as part of the Graphikslava crew.

Aburtov has worked in the comic book industry for more than eleven years. In that time, he has illustrated popular characters such as Wolverine, Iron Man, Blade, and the Punisher. Recently, Aburtov started his own illustration studio called Graphikslava. He lives in Monterrey, Mexico, with his daughter, Ilka, and his beloved wife. Aburtov enjoys spending his spare time with family and friends.

Jaymes Reed has operated the company Digital-CAPS: Comic Book Lettering since 2003. He has done lettering for many publishers, most notably Avatar Press. He's also the only letterer working with Inception Strategies, an Aboriginal-Australian publisher that develops social comics with public service messages for the Australian government. Jaymes is a 2012 and 2013 Shel Dorf Award Nominee.

MORE SPORTS.
MORE ACTION.
MORE VICTORIES.

READ ALL THE JAKE MADDOX GRAPHIC NOVELS!

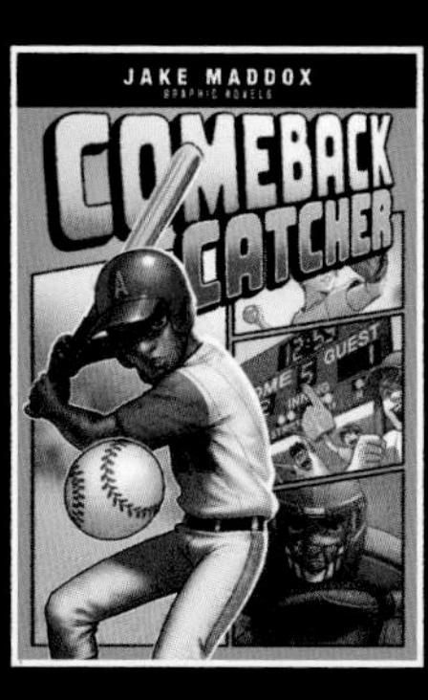

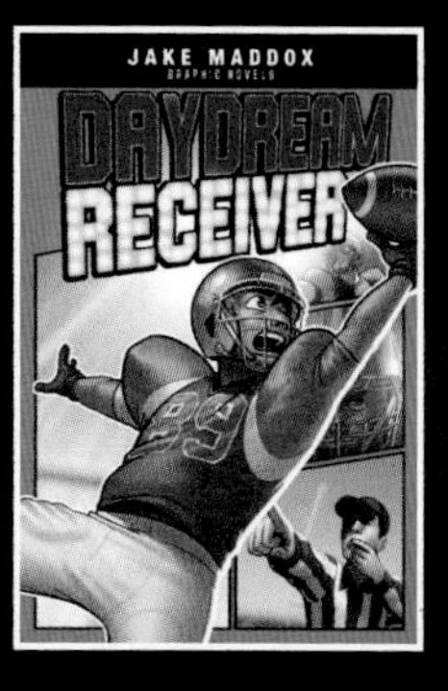

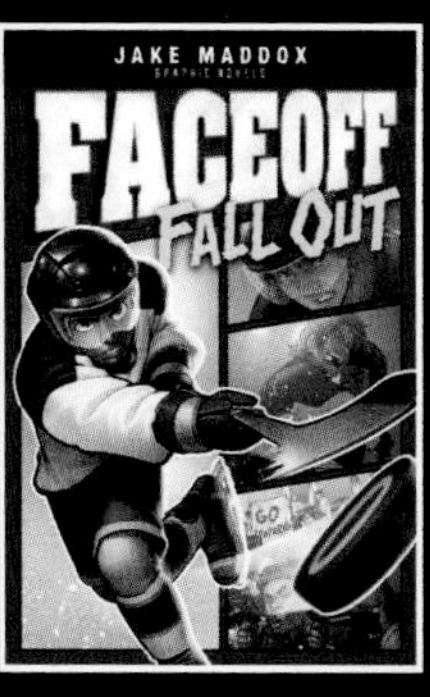

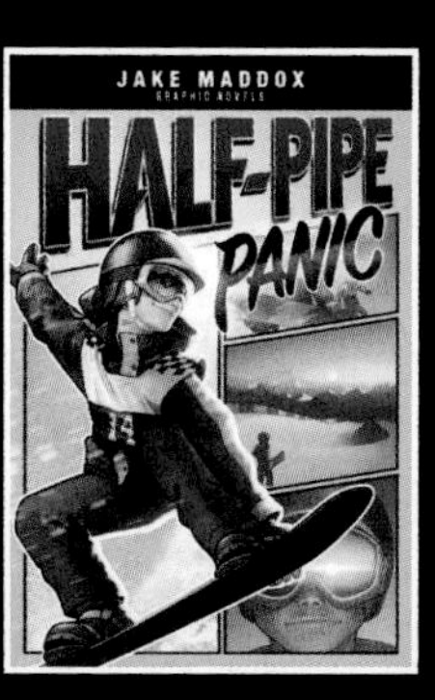

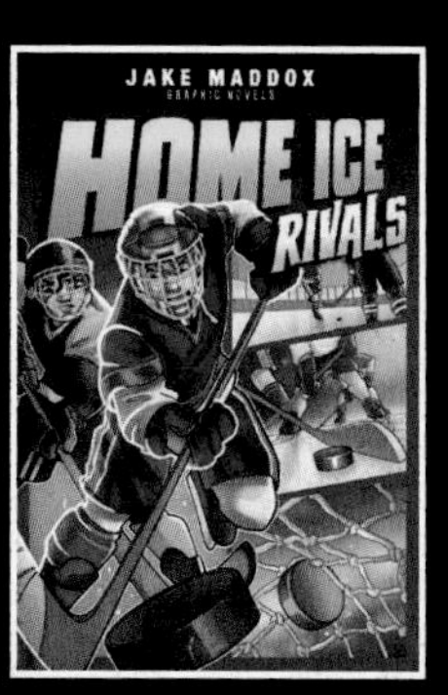

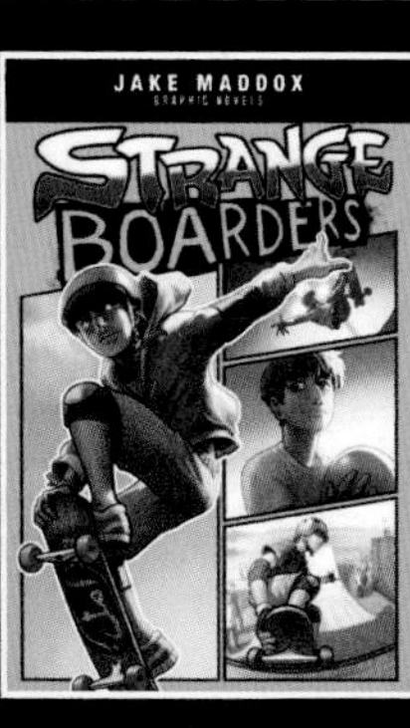

Published by Stone Arch Books, an imprint of Capstone.
1710 Roe Crest Drive
North Mankato, Minnesota 56003
capstonepub.com

Library of Congress Cataloging-in-Publication Data
is available at the Library of Congress website.
ISBN: 9781663934178 (paperback)
ISBN: 9781663934161 (ebook PDF)

Summary: From bestselling author Jake Maddox comes a collection that brings together three action-packed basketball stories into one full-color graphic novel. Cheer on young athletes as they overcome challenges to achieve victory both on the court and in life.

Editors: Aaron Sautter, Abby Huff
Designer: Brann Garvey
A Taste for Victory and *Basketball Camp Champ* cover art
by Berenice Muñiz
Double Scribble cover art by Fern Cano

Printed and bound in the United States of America. PO4270